BAXTER'S BOOK

Hrefna Bragadottir

nosy crow

BAXTER'S BOOK

First published in 2016

by Nosy Crow Ltd.

The Crow's Nest,

10a Lant Street,

London SE1 1QR

www.nosycrow.com

ISBN 978 0 85763 521 1 (HB)

ISBN 978 0 85763 522 8 (PB)

Text and illustration copyright

© Hrefna Bragadottir 2016

The right of Hrefna Bragadottir

to be identified

as the author and illustrator

of this work has been asserted.

All rights reserved

A CIP catalogue record for this book

is available from the British Library.

Printed in China by Imago.

Papers used by Nosy Crow are made from

wood grown in sustainable forests.

1 3 5 7 9 8 6 4 2 (HB)

1 3 5 7 9 8 6 4 2 (PB)

For my dad,
Bragi Halldórsson,
who taught me never to
give up on my dreams.

GIANT GIRAFFE

THE SLUG IN THE MUG

I love books!

I love books about
scary wolves . . .

books about
brave lions . . .

roar

books about
cuddly bears . . .

and books about
cute little rabbits.

If **only** I could be in a book, too!

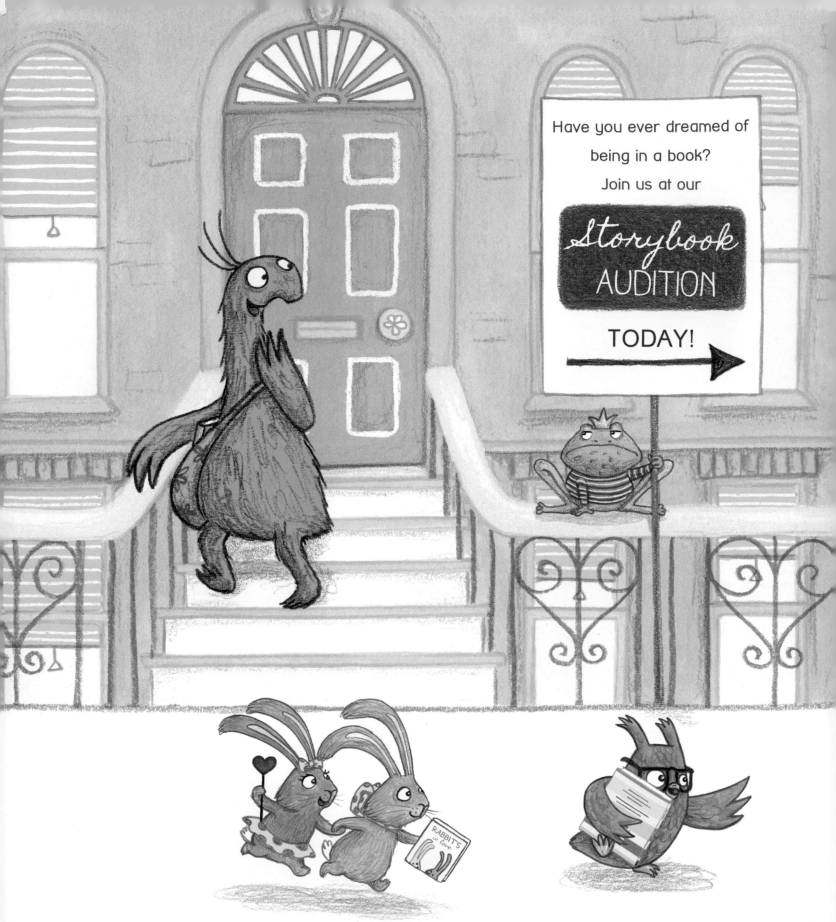

The sign on the audition poster reads:

Have you ever dreamed of being in a book? Join us at our

Storybook AUDITION

TODAY!

Hang on! That sign wasn't there before.
Storybook audition?
That's it! This is my moment!

And it looks like I'd better hurry!

It's a very long queue! And everyone here
has been in a book before except me.

Wow – I can't **wait** to get started.
I have so many great talents!

And they've asked me to go first!

I can sing . . .

I can dance . . .

I'm great at gymnastics . . .

and my acting is very good.

I'm just **perfect** for a book.

I've never seen anything like that in a book before!

VERY ODD!

What an unusual creature!

IS IT A BIRD?

WELL, I don't think it's quite what we're looking for!

NEXT!

What if I'm not good enough
to be in a book?

Wolf says if I want
to be in a book,
I need to be
scary!

But I just feel
silly.

Ha Haah!
Hee hee! Haha!

Bear says
if I want
to be in a book,
I need to be
cuddly!

But I don't
know how.

And Rabbit says
if I want to be in
a book, I need to
be **cute!**

But . . .

I'm not
scary like Wolf.

I'm not
brave like Lion.

And I'm not
cuddly like Bear
or **cute**
like Rabbit.

It's **too** hard.
I don't want to be
in a book anymore!
I just want
to go home!

But . . . what's this?

I'm in a book?!

My wish came true.